這本書是屬於我摯愛的：

This book is for my dear：

Author's background

Dr. Y.F.H. Angie
National Taiwan Junior and Senior High School Teacher's Certificate
Promoter of Montessori Teaching Methods
美國加州柏克萊大學博士　/　台灣中等學校教師合格證書　/　蒙特梭利教材設計研究者

作者的話

蒙特梭利教材方法重視兒童及青少年獨立思考、發展，
在有限度的自由下給予心理和社會性發展的尊重，
本書爲眞實故事改編，
融入人本主義精神與透過循序漸進方式讓兒童及青少年了解交友與同儕影響的重要性，
進而健全擇友與交友能力。"尊重"爲反霸凌運動的先驅，
"你遇到的困難，別人也會遇到，在遇到困難時，
如何面對與尋找支持的力量"，是人的一生中皆需要學習的課題，
本書適合3歲以上、青少年至成人階段的讀者閱讀，
邀請您一起重視教育心理學，健全兒童及青少年心理結構。

Author's words

The Montessori teaching method emphasizes independent thinking
and development of children and adolescents, and respects psychological and social development.
This book is adapted from a real story, incorporating the spirit of humanism and allowing children
and adolescents to understand the importance of making friends and
peer influence, and then improve their ability to choose friends and make friends.
"Respect" is the driver of the anti-bullying movement.
"The difficulties you encounter, others will also encounter. When encountering difficulties,
how to face them and find the strength to overcome them?" are subjects that we all must keep
learning through our whole lives. The book with its many vibrant pictures is suitable
for children over the age of 3, as well as being relevant to teenagers and adults.
You are invited to pay attention to educational psychology
and improve the psychological structure of children and teenagers.

出版商的話

樂木文化隸屬樂木國際貿易有限公司於2022年成立樂木國際文化事業部
支持兒童與青少年發展、重視人本精神、提升國際交流與各式產業文化。
邀請您一起做公益，讓老有所終，壯有所用，幼有所長，
矜寡孤獨，廢疾者，皆有所養。

From the publisher

La Morongo Culture and Charity is affiliated with La Morongo International Trading Co., Ltd.
In 2022, the department of La Morongo Culture and Charity was established to support
the development of children and young people,
pay attention to the humanistic spirit,
and enhance international exchanges and various industrial cultures.
We invite you to join us in helping increase public welfare together,
so that the old will be able to live with grace,
the strong will find their uses,
the young will grow strong,
and the widowed or lonely and disabled or sick will be supported.

小松鼠準備到美國去上學了，
美國是一個遙遠的地方，小松鼠跟爸爸媽媽道別。
The little squirrel is going to America to go to school.
The United States is a far away place.
The little squirrel says goodbye to her parents.

爸媽：一個人要多保重喔！
Take care, my sweet heart.

爸爸、媽媽，再見，
我去上學囉，我會想念你們的
Goodbye, dad and mom.
I am going to school. I will miss you.

好ㄏㄠˇ漂ㄆㄧㄠˋ亮ㄌㄧㄤˋ的ㄉㄜ學ㄒㄩㄝˊ校ㄒㄧㄠˋ，我ㄨㄛˇ會ㄏㄨㄟˋ認ㄖㄣˋ眞ㄓㄣ學ㄒㄩㄝˊ習ㄒㄧˊ的ㄉㄜ。
Such a beautiful school, I will study hard.

小松鼠在學校認識的第一個朋友是狐狸學妹.
他們一起玩、一起吃飯、一起坐車、一起買菜。
The first friend the squirrel makes is Miss Fox.
They play, eat, carpool, and shop together.

很高興認識你，我們一起玩吧！
Nice to meet you.　Let's play together.

狐狸學妹是一個熱情的人。
Miss Fox is an enthusiastic person.
When she goes out to play, she will think of the little
squirrel, and send postcards to the little squirrel.

給小松鼠：
我出去玩了很開心，
想到你， 你是我最好的朋友。

狐狸敬上

To: Little Squirrel

I am on an outing, very happy,
and I miss you.
You are my best friend.

From: Miss Fox

然而，每次見面的時候，狐狸學妹總是逼問私人的問題，告訴狐狸學妹的事情總是被講出去，狐狸學妹告訴了所有的人，就算小松鼠覺得需要保密也還是被講了出去…

However, every time they meet, Miss Fox asks the little squirrel personal questions. The things the little squirrel tells Miss Fox always become public knowledge, although the little squirrel prefers privacy....

狐狸學妹把小松鼠的秘密到處散播。
正義人士跑來告誡小松鼠狐狸學妹其實很壞。
Miss Fox spreads the little squirrel's secrets everywhere. Righteous people come to warn the little squirrel that Miss Fox actually is bad.

嗨，大家，讓我告訴你們小松鼠的秘密吧，
我知道秘密，因為我是小松鼠最好的朋友嘛，哈哈哈！
Hey everyone, let me tell you about the little squirrel's secrets.
I know them, because I am her best friend, hahaha!

小松鼠，你要小心狐狸學妹，她到處講妳八卦。
[順便讓你知道，我是果子狸，我是一個訪問學者]
Little squirrel, you need to be careful of Miss Fox.
She is spreading gossip about you.
[For your information, I am a civet. I'm a visiting scholar.

小松鼠很傷心。
Little Squirrel feels heartbroken.

狐狸學妹是我真正的朋友嗎？
Is Miss Fox my real friend?

有些人會傷害你， 有時候並不是你的錯，
原因是他們內心裡有陰影。
遇到陰影面積很大的人， 我們不要靠得太近。

When somebody hurts you, it sometimes is not your fault.
It's because they have a dark side.
When you meet people with a large dark side, don't be too close.

狐狸學妹的內心陰影面積：½ 個圓
The inner dark side area of Miss Fox: ½ of the circle.

過了一段時間，
小松鼠又認識了新朋友， 是一隻小刺蝟。
每次刺蝟需要幫助的時候， 小松鼠總是伸出援手。
他們互相幫助。

After a while, the little squirrel meets a new friend,
a little hedgehog. Every time Hedgehog needs help,
the little squirrel always helps him. They help each other.

小松鼠跟刺蝟一起探險，一起唸書，一起玩耍。
他們在一起很開心，然而…

The little squirrel and Hedgehog explore together,
study together, and play everywhere.
They are happy together, however …

當刺蝟自信心低落的時候， 他的刺會豎起來。
刺蝟並不是故意的， 他天性如此。
當他們兩個人太靠近的時候， 小松鼠就會被刺到。
When Hedgehog has low self-esteem, his spikes stand up.
The hedgehog doesn't mean to do this, it's just his nature.
When they are too close, the little squirrel gets poked.

好痛.It hurts!

豎滿刺的刺蝟說：
妳為什麼要對我這麼好？
如果我越來越喜歡妳怎麼辦？
The spiky hedgehog says,
"Why are you so nice to me?
What if I like you more and more?"

小松鼠不管說什麼都沒有用， 小松鼠一直受傷。
No matter what the little squirrel says, it does not work.
The little squirrel keeps getting hurt.

真的是太莫名其妙了！
自卑感高的人也會有很大的心理陰影面積。

It's really inexplicable! People with a high sense of inferiority also have a large psychological shadow area.

當他們感到害怕或是自卑時， 他們會縮成一團球，
全身長滿長長的刺， 刺向靠近他們的人。

When they are afraid or feel inferior, they will curl up into a ball, grow long spikes all over their bodies, and stab people close to them.

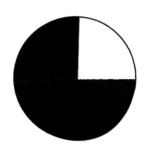

刺蝟的內心陰影面積：3/4 個圓

The inner dark side area of Hedgehog：3/4 of the circle.

你要知道別人傷害你並不是你的錯，
是他們的天性使然。 當你試著改變他們或靠近他們時，
你會受傷。 你有這樣的朋友嗎？
他們是你真正的朋友嗎？ 你真正需要做的事是：
遠離那些擁有過大陰影面積的人，
在草原上持續尋找白色面積大一點的人"

You have to know that it is not your fault that some people hurt you, rather their nature. Whether you try to change them or try to get close to them, you will be hurt. Do you have such a friend?
Are they really your friend? What you really should do is：
"Stay away from people with too large of a dark side.
Keep looking for folks in the grassland with large bright parts inside."

高大的長頸鹿說：
"當你有一天想要回來， 可以回到我身邊。
我們可以一起開心地吃葉子就像現在一樣"。

The tall giraffe says
"When you want to come back one day, you can return to me.
We can eat leaves happily together like now!"

真正的朋友是：
他們會尊重你。
他們會一如繼往地等待與陪伴你。
站在他們的肩膀上，
你可以看到更高更遠的地方。
你有這樣的朋友嗎？

A real friend is like this:
They will respect you.
They will wait for, and accompany you
always. Standing on their shoulders,
you can see higher and farther.
Do you have such a friend?

嘿～ 老朋友，我來看你了，好久不見了，你好嗎？
Hey old friend, I came to see you. Long time, no see. How are you?

我好想你
I miss you so much.

小松鼠帶著他遠道而來的老朋友到處看看。
Little Squirrel took her old friend from afar to look around.

眞正的朋友是：
他們有很大的白色面積。
他們不需要依賴你去填補他們的陰影，
因為他們的內心已經足夠強大了。
你有這樣的朋友嗎？

A real friend is like this:
They have a large bright area.
They don't need to rely on you to fill up their dark side,
because their inner self is already strong enough.
Do you have such a friend?

在你的一生中，　會遇到各式困境。
你遇到的困境其他人也一樣會遇到。
我們必須努力尋找內心白色面積比黑色面積大的朋友。
而當我們的內心擁有很大的白色面積時，
也就越容易吸引到跟我們一樣內心強大的人。
你是一個這樣的朋友嗎？

In your life, you will encounter all kinds of difficulties.
The difficulties you encounter will also be encountered by others.
We must work hard to find friends with more bright areas
in their hearts than dark parts.
When our own inner self has large bright areas inside,
it is easier to attract strong people like us.
Are you such a friend?

蒙特梭利與人本精神

小松鼠上學記

Dr. Y.F.H. Angie

出版 / 樂木國際文化事業部

統編 / 60311767

地址 / 台中市南區美和街106號5F-2

電話 / 04-22630179　傳眞 / 04-22630179

平裝版

定價 / 台幣350元

初版 2023/09/01

樂木國際文化事業部支持兒童與青少年發展

您的捐款我們將以贈書的方式支援需要幫助的兒童與青少年團體

捐款方法

中華郵政

劃撥帳號：22868631

收款戶名：樂木國際貿易有限公司

請於劃撥單備註區寫上： 1.受贈者名稱 / 地址 / 電話　 2.捐款人名稱 / 統編 / email

我們將幫您直接寄書給受贈者

＊捐款金額將以email提供發票或捐款收據供抵稅使用

＊We support humanistic education concerning childrens' and teenagers' behavior.

To offer a donation in the USA area, please contact: La.Morongo.Co@gmail.com

你³有³哪³些Ⅰ朋²友ⅠⅤ？ 畫ⅤⅤ出ⅠⅤ你³最ⅠⅤ喜Ⅰ歡ⅠⅤ的²朋²友ⅠⅤ吧³：

Who are your friends ? Draw them here :